More About the Kane Family
by Judith Caseley

HARRY AND ARNEY

CHLOE IN THE KNOW

STARRING DOROTHY KANE

HURRICANE HARRY

JUDITH CASELEY

Dorothy's Darkest Days

Greenwillow Books, New York

Library of Congress Cataloging-in-Publication Data
Caseley, Judith.
Dorothy's darkest days / by Judith Caseley.
p.   cm.
Summary: Dorothy's boisterous life with her parents,
two brothers, and sister is suddenly changed when
something tragic happens to a classmate of hers, but
she finds that things eventually do return to normal.
ISBN 0-688-13422-X
[1. Brothers and sisters—Fiction.
2. Family life—Fiction.
3. Death—Fiction.]   I. Title.
PZ7.C2677Do   1997
[Fic]—dc21
96-39175   CIP   AC

For SCH,
with love again

Contents

1 ○ Dorothy's Dark Day   1

2 ○ Dorothy's Dog Days   23

3 ○ The Lady with the Lamp   41

4 ○ Dorothy's Tragedy   65

5 ○ Dorothy's Light   89

6 ○ Toto Rides Again   98

Dorothy's Darkest Days

1

Dorothy's Dark Day

DOROTHY LOVED HER baby brother Arney's fat pink cheeks. She loved his big blue eyes that her mother said would probably turn hazel when he got a little older. She loved his little pink toes and his tiny clenched fingers that made him look like a miniature boxer.

When Mama put Arney in Dorothy's lap, she loved the gurgling sound he made when he was contented and the widening of his eyes as he caught a glimpse of his big sister.

"Babies love children," said Mrs. Kane, arranging her daughter's arms around Arney. "He squirms," she cautioned Dorothy, "so hold him close. I'm going to start dinner."

Harry settled himself on the couch next to Dorothy. "He's strong like me," he said, holding up his own arm and clenching his six-year-old muscles.

"Yeah, right." Dorothy's older sister, Chloe, put down her math notebook. "Muscles of marshmallow."

"I love marshmallow!" said Harry.

Chloe snorted. "Do you remember the time you ate a whole jar of Marshmallow Fluff?" she asked him.

Dorothy made a face. "Please," she said, jiggling Arney as he started to whimper. "It's almost suppertime!"

Chloe ignored her. "You threw up all night long," she reminded Harry.

"I did not!" said Harry crossly.

Arney turned up the volume, and Dorothy jiggled more briskly. "You two are making me sick," she said.

Chloe was relentless. "Don't you remember? Mama put a wastepaper basket in your bed so that you wouldn't miss if you had to run to the bathroom."

Arney screeched loudly in a higher register than before, and Mama sailed into the room.

"Let me take him," said Mrs. Kane, scooping the baby out of Dorothy's arms, too late to prevent a creamy deposit from landing on his sister's shoulder.

Dorothy loved her baby brother's pink little cheeks and tiny boxerlike fists and his gurgling sounds. But she hated, absolutely hated, when he spit up on her.

"Yuck," said Dorothy, wrinkling up her nose in disgust.

"He got back at you for saying mean things about his big brother," said Harry.

"I didn't say a word!" said Dorothy. "Chloe was the one!"

"Mama told you to put a cloth over your shoulder," Chloe said smugly.

3

"I did, Dorothy," Mama called over her shoulder as she exited with a wailing Arney.

Harry had to have the last word. "Arney wants to be like me," he yelled after his sister as she followed Mama down the hallway. "He spit up, just like I did!"

Dorothy went into her bedroom. She peeled off her soiled shirt and pulled one of her favorite books off the shelf. The Heavenly Hill twins never got spewed on, she was sure of that. They wore crisp new clothes in the latest styles. They had no screeching brothers, baby sized or Harry sized. Their lives were simple and uncomplicated, not yucky and annoying like hers.

When the new baby had arrived, Harry had acted like a pain from the start. He thought he had owned Arney, just because they were both boys. Harry called their bedroom "the boys' room," as if it were some kind of barricade against the girls in the family. Harry had given up his B.O.N.G. club (Boys Only, No Girls) just a few weeks ago. But had he given up the attitude that boys were better than girls? Dorothy didn't think so.

4

She flicked through the twins book and found her place. It was prom time in Heavenly Hill, but reading was impossible with Arney screaming in the background and Harry emitting some weird kind of whooping noises that sounded just like the cartoons he watched.

Dorothy slipped on a fresh shirt and left her room. Her mother was back in the living room, doing the dipping dance as she tried to calm Arney.

"What's that?" said Dorothy, pointing to a blanket wrapped so snugly around Arney that it reminded Dorothy of the Egyptian mummies they were studying in school.

"What's what?" said Mrs. Kane, bobbing up and down as Arney sobbed.

Dorothy moved closer. "It's my baby blanket," she said, fingering the soft material. "I remember the cute little bunnies on it."

"I know," said her mother in between bobs. "You don't need it anymore."

"I do so," said Dorothy hotly. "I can use it when I play with my doll Samantha."

Mrs. Kane sighed. "Blankets cost money, Dorothy. I am not about to run out and buy new blankets for your brother."

Dorothy glared at her mother. "Why can't you use Harry's?" she said.

"Harry's blankets were ripped to shreds a long time ago," said Mrs. Kane in an exasperated tone.

"What about Chloe's blankets?" said Dorothy, refusing to back down although it was obvious that her mother's nostrils were beginning to flare.

"Dorothy," her mother said sharply, "when Chloe was born, I bought her some baby blankets. The good ones went to you, and then to Harry. Whatever survived has gone to Arney." Mrs. Kane shifted Arney into his second favorite motion, rocking him back and forth.

"It's only a silly blanket," Chloe called from the kitchen.

"You got brand-new blankets when you were born!" Dorothy yelled back. Hands on her hips, she said to her mother, "I want my blanket."

Harry sailed into the room, arms flapping. "I want my blanky, I want my blanky," he whined.

"Harry, Chloe, please mind your own business." Mrs. Kane's voice was raspy. "Dorothy, the subject is closed."

Dorothy's temper flared. "It isn't fair!" she cried. "I should get to keep my own baby blanket!"

"Mrs. Ehrenkrantz has a dog who sleeps on blankets," Harry declared. "He's an Irish settler."

"Irish setter," Chloe called from the kitchen.

"Bed wetter," Harry called back.

"Look who's talking," chided Dorothy. "You wet your bed a month ago."

"Harry's a sound sleeper," said Mrs. Kane, rocking and rocking. "Are Arney's eyes closing?" she said in a low voice, as if the baby could understand English and would open his eyes immediately, just to spite her.

"He's going," said Harry.

"They're closed," said Dorothy grouchily.

"Good," said Mrs. Kane, lowering the baby into his carrier. "Harry, let's work on your homework now while I try to start dinner. Go get some magazines and look for pictures that start with the letter *P*. Dorothy, why don't you start studying your spelling words?"

"I'm hungry," said Dorothy, following her mother into the kitchen. "Could I have a cookie first?"

Harry sped into the kitchen waving a stack of magazines. "I'll have some puh-puh-*P* for 'popcorn,' " he said. "Or some puh-puh-*P* for 'pretzels'."

"You can have a *C* for 'carrot' or an *A* for 'apple,' " said Mrs. Kane.

"Or a *V* for 'vegetables,' " said Dorothy, brightening at the chance to help Harry with his alphabet book instead of studying her spelling.

Harry flicked through the pages of a magazine. "I don't see any *P*'s," he said glumly.

"I have an idea," said Dorothy, rummaging in the kitchen cabinet above the sink. "You can use Mama's coupons!" she said triumphantly, pulling out an envelope stuffed with newspaper and magazine clippings. "Here, Harry," she added, "a coupon for popcorn!"

"At fifty cents off," said Mrs. Kane, smiling. "Tape it in your book, honey."

Harry found a coupon for frozen pizza (at seventy-five cents off) and a picture of a blueberry Pop Tart (at thirty-five cents off). Mrs. Kane put her foot down when he found a picture of a sparkling white toilet on a coupon for toilet bowl cleaner.

"The word 'toilet' does not begin with a P," she informed Harry.

" 'Toilet' begins with a T," said Dorothy.

" 'Pee-pee' begins with the letter P," Harry chortled. "You make pee-pee in the toilet and that's the letter P."

"Harry Kane!" his mother said, laughing. "You are not handing in a picture of a toilet with imaginary pee-pee in it."

"How about poo-poo?" said Harry.

Mrs. Kane rolled her eyes. "Let's leave the bathroom world out of our alphabet notebook, okay, Harry?"

"The word 'pet' begins with *P*," said Dorothy. "You could draw a picture of Personality! Personality begins with the letter *P*, too!"

"I want to do it by myself!" said Harry, covering his ears with his hands.

Mrs. Kane sighed deeply. "Don't help him anymore, Dorothy. Let him do it by himself."

"Oh, fine," said Dorothy, imitating her mother's sigh as she opened her knapsack and removed her spelling book.

Harry ran to the cupboard and took out a jar of peanuts. "Puh-puh-puh-peanuts!" he said gleefully. "Can I paste a peanut in my book?"

Mrs. Kane let him tape one peanut into his book, but when Harry begged to be allowed to tape down his pencil, she shook her head.

"At least you know your letter *P*," she told him.

"It's my turn," said Chloe, holding a page of fraction problems under her mother's nose. "I'm having trouble with number seven."

"Heaven help me," said Mrs. Kane, sitting down at the kitchen table and studying the paper. She scribbled something on a napkin and held it up to Chloe.

"I don't think that's correct," said Chloe, pointing to the paper. "It's multiple choice, and your answer isn't even on the page!"

When Arney let out a peep in the other room, Mrs. Kane's nostrils flared again and she mumbled something under her breath about the baby waking up and what a short nap he'd taken and how she hadn't even started supper yet. She handed the worksheet back to Chloe. "You'll have to wait for your father to come home," Mrs. Kane said tensely. "Math was never my strongest subject."

Dorothy waved her list of spelling words in the air. "Can you quiz me now?" she asked her mother.

"Right about now, Dorothy, my head is spinning," said her mother. "Let's work on your words after supper."

"What are we having for dinner?" Dorothy asked quite innocently, as there wasn't a sign of a pot boiling or an empty box of macaroni and cheese or a whiff of anything coming from the oven.

"Leftovers," said Mrs. Kane, running into the living room as Arney peeped for a second time. She crouched over the baby, whispering softly as she jiggled the carrier. Arney's eyes fluttered open for a moment and closed again as he settled back into sleep. "You look like hungry vultures!" she said to the children, who had followed her into the living room. "I promise I'll start dinner now."

"Vultures eat dead things!" said Chloe, making a face.

"We're more like baby robins waiting for their mothers to feed them," said Dorothy, opening and closing her mouth as if it were a beak.

"Worms!" Harry cheeped like a bird. "We want our worms!"

Mrs. Kane laughed. "You're too much, Harry."

"You always laugh at Harry," Dorothy said grumpily.

"Hello!" said Mr. Kane, striding into the room. "I'm home, thank heavens."

"Shhh!" said Dorothy, holding a finger up to her lips.

"Quiet!" said Harry, pointing to his sleeping brother.

"Did you pick up the milk?" said Mrs. Kane.

"No, I did not," said Mr. Kane in a voice that sounded as grumpy as Dorothy's. "It's good to have you home, dear. How was your day, Dad? Are you tired, Dad?"

Mrs. Kane retreated into the kitchen, and the living room was quiet.

Dorothy squinted at her father. "Are you being sarcastic?" she said.

"He is," said Chloe, appearing at her sister's side.

Mr. Kane bent over Arney. "Look at this beautiful sweet doll," he murmured.

Dorothy didn't know why she did what she did at that particular moment, but she stooped low next to her father, took hold of her soft bunny blanket, and pulled.

Arney rolled to one side and bumped his round cheek against the side of the carrier. He started to wail.

"It's my blanket," said Dorothy, leaning over the

carrier to see if Arney was all right. Her father moved quickly, shoving Dorothy aside so forcefully that she landed on her knees.

"You pushed me!" cried Dorothy, tears springing to her eyes.

"You pushed her!" said Harry, eyes wide.

"He pushed you!" said Chloe, as if Dorothy didn't know it.

Dorothy's father scooped up Arney and peered at his face. It was clear and unblemished. Mr. Kane's own brow was furrowed. His large jaw was clenched. He didn't say a word.

"What happened?" said Mrs. Kane, hurrying to Arney's side.

"Daddy pushed Dorothy," Chloe announced.

"Dorothy wanted her blanket," piped up Harry.

"She yanked it right off the baby, and he practically flipped over," said Mr. Kane in a low voice.

"I did not!" cried Dorothy, sobbing as she ran to her room.

Dorothy flopped across the bed and buried her face in the pillow. Her tears wet the pale blue flowers that decorated the pillowcase. One knee was hurting, and Dorothy wondered if it was bleeding. It would serve her father right if she had to go to the hospital and get stitches like Harry had gotten when he'd jumped on Mr. Tuttle's new thorny bushes by mistake. Maybe then her father would stop worrying about Arney and start worrying about his middle child. Except that it occurred to Dorothy that she was no longer the middle child, now that Arney was born.

There was a knock on the door. Dorothy put the pillow over her head and lay silent.

"It's me," said her mother. "May I come in?"

"No," said Dorothy, pressing the pillow down around her ears as her mother appeared in the doorway.

"Your father shouldn't have pushed you," began her mother, placing a hand on Dorothy's shoulder.

Dorothy didn't say a word.

"He feels bad about it," said Mrs. Kane.

Dorothy didn't move.

"It's just that Daddy was afraid that Arney had been hurt," her mother explained.

"I would never hurt Arney!" Dorothy said fiercely, flinging aside the pillow.

"I know that," said Mrs. Kane gently.

A familiar wailing sound reached Dorothy's ears. Her mother stiffened. She reminded Dorothy of Mr. Ritter's cocker spaniel, whose ears twitched when he heard his name called. Mrs. Kane's ears were twitching now, but she didn't get up.

"Won't you come eat with us?" said Mrs. Kane.

Dorothy was about to speak when the wailing grew louder. Her mother called loudly, "Do you have him, Hank?"

The crying continued and Dorothy's mother shifted on the bed. "Are you holding him?" she cried.

"I think he's hungry," Mr. Kane called back.

Mrs. Kane stood up. "Come and join us for supper," she said, patting Dorothy once more before she turned to go.

"Mama?" said Dorothy.

"Yes, honey?" said her mother, turning back.

"How come you always laugh at Harry's jokes and not at mine?"

Mrs. Kane sucked in air and let it whistle through her nose. "Oh, Dorothy," she said. "Is that really true?"

"Yes," said Dorothy. "It is."

Mrs. Kane thought for a moment. "Maybe it's that he's my youngest," she said. "At least he was until Arney was born. I still think of him as the baby."

"I'd like to be the baby sometime," said Dorothy, laying her face back down on her pillow. "Everybody loves babies."

"You're my baby, too," said Mrs. Kane, kissing Dorothy's head before she turned to leave.

Dorothy listened to the click of the door closing. She heard the beeping sound of the microwave oven going off. Her stomach was beginning to rumble and Mama had mentioned leftovers for dinner, which probably meant that it wasn't a honey-glazed chicken day. It felt much more like a reheated Chinese food day, lo mein to be exact, with steamed broccoli as the healthy part of the meal.

There was another knock on the door. A steady sound, not as loud and pounding as Harry's brand of knocking, not as fast and light as Chloe's.

"Dorothy?" said her father, his voice so low that she could hardly hear him. "May I come in?"

"I guess," muttered Dorothy.

Mr. Kane sat down on the bed in exactly the same spot where her mother had sat. He didn't pat her shoulder. "I'm sorry, honey," he said.

"You pushed me," Dorothy said under her breath.

"I know I did," said her father. "I was wrong to do that."

Dorothy sat up. "Do you remember when Benny Spignolli was hitting me with snowballs?" she said accusingly. "And we had him over to dinner and he told us that his father was a boxer, and he said he would show us how to pack a mean wallop?"

Mr. Kane smiled and took Dorothy's hand. "I remember," he said.

Dorothy pulled her hand away. "And Chloe was studying Mahatma Gandhi who didn't believe in violence, and we said that our family didn't believe in violence. No pushing, punching, or hitting, you told us. Use your words, you said."

"I did," said Mr. Kane. "That's what I told you. And I still believe it." Dorothy's father shook his head. "I made a mistake, honey."

"How come you had to make a mistake with me?" said Dorothy. "Why couldn't it be with Harry or Chloe?"

Mr. Kane raised an eyebrow. "I hit your brother once, Dorothy. Do you remember when he was little and he went through a biting phase? He was mad about something, and I don't know what happened. I just remember that he bit me. And I was so surprised and shocked that I hit him."

"What did Harry do?" said Dorothy.

"He hit me right back," said Mr. Kane. "And I vowed then and there that I would never hit any of my children again, because that was the wrong message. Hitting was no solution. So I'm hoping that you, my smart, darling middle child, will be more grown-up than your father, and forgive me."

Dorothy looked into her father's eyes, which were very serious and intent as his eyeglasses slipped down his nose. "I'm not the middle child anymore," she said.

Mr. Kane laughed. "So you're not," he said, pulling Dorothy to her feet.

"And I hurt my knee," said Dorothy, limping across the room.

"Into the emergency room," said Mr. Kane, leading Dorothy into the bathroom. "Let Dr. Kane have a look."

Dorothy's father examined her knee. "It's pink," he declared, taking a tube of antiseptic cream out of the cabinet and dabbing a bit on the skin. Dorothy could see a small bald spot on the top of her father's head as he taped a Band-Aid across her knee. She touched the spot with her finger.

"That's good luck," said Mr. Kane, smiling. "I used to rub the top of my father's head when I was little. He told me it was lucky."

"Did your father ever hit you?" said Dorothy.

Mr. Kane shook his head. "Never in my life," he said, taking Dorothy's hand as they walked into the kitchen.

"Do I smell honey-glazed chicken?" Dorothy said hopefully.

"You wish," said her father. "It's leftover Chinese food."

Dorothy sighed. "I was afraid of that," she said, sitting down in her usual place next to Chloe and tucking into the bowl of reheated lo mein that her mother put in front of her.

"I saved a fortune cookie for you," said Harry, holding out his hand.

"It's broken," said Dorothy as she took the cookie and it fell apart on the table.

"Read the fortune," said Harry excitedly.

Dorothy pulled a thin slip of paper out of the cookie half. On the paper, using a black felt-tip marker, someone with six-year-old penmanship had written a message.

"What does it say?" asked Chloe, smiling.

Dorothy read the strip of paper out loud. "It says, 'We love Dorothy.'"

"That's one smart fortune cookie," said Mr. Kane.

"It sure is," said Mrs. Kane, Arney peeping in her arms.

"Confucius wrote it," said Harry, beaming. "He was a very smart Chinese man. Almost as smart as I am."

Dorothy started to laugh. "You're funny, Harry," she said, and she ate her cookie.

2

Dorothy's Dog Days

DOROTHY PUT DOWN the book she was reading and announced to Chloe, "I wish I were a twin. In my Heavenly Hill book, Jenna and Jessica are twins, and they get to do all sorts of neat things."

"That's because the book is fiction," said Chloe, in the know-it-all tone of a big sister. "Great stuff always happens to people who aren't real."

"Great stuff happens to me," said Harry. "I found a bat in Grandma's apartment."

"Gross stuff happens to you," said Chloe, "not great stuff."

23

Dorothy laughed. "It's true, Harry. You got stitches in your leg, and that was pretty gross."

Chloe bit into an apple. "Not to mention killing off your turtle," she said in between munches.

"I didn't kill Personality," said Harry hotly. "The washing machine and the dryer did that!"

"He's right," said Dorothy, patting Harry on the head and watching him twitch away. "It wasn't Harry's fault." Dorothy picked up her book again and fanned through the pages. "Still, twins get to wear each other's clothes and they pull tricks on people and they're never lonely."

Mrs. Kane walked into the kitchen with Arney hanging over her shoulder. "Are you telling me that you're lonely, Dorothy?" Arney squawked loudly. "With all of us around?"

Chloe took another bite of her apple. "You can wear my clothes if you want," she said. She turned toward her mother. "We need to buy more green apples, Mama. They're better than the red ones."

Mama touched noses with Arney. "Make a note, Mr. Secretary. Chloe likes Granny Smith apples."

"I don't," said Dorothy, making a face. "She likes everything green. I wouldn't be caught dead in those yellow and orange and green clothes of yours, Chloe. And those green apples are sour!"

"What's so great about those blue and red and black clothes of yours?" said Chloe.

"We could never be twins," said Dorothy, shaking her head. "We're too different."

"And you look different," said Harry. "Chloe looks like the elf on the cereal box and Dorothy looks like Mama without those wrinkles."

"Thanks a lot, Harry," said Mrs. Kane, putting a pacifier into Arney's mouth. He sucked noisily on it.

"He looks like a pig," said Harry, screwing up his nose.

Arney spit out the pacifier.

"See?" said Harry triumphantly. "He agrees with me."

Chloe rolled her eyes and whispered to Dorothy, "Let's get out of here."

"Put away your homework, girls," said Mrs.

Kane as Dorothy and Chloe pushed away from the table. "And come back in time to make salad for supper." She turned to Harry. "You, young man, can pick up the pacifier for me and rinse it under the faucet."

The sisters gathered up their books and put them in their bedrooms.

"Let's go to the backyard," whispered Dorothy, sliding open the doors. "Quietly, so Harry won't follow."

Dorothy and Chloe breathed in the late afternoon spring air. "I think springtime is my favorite season," said Dorothy, bending to pat the yellow head of a flower. "I love tulips."

"I thought you hated yellow," said Chloe. "I like the smell of roses better. Tulips don't really smell."

Harry poked his head out the sliding doors. "Who smells?" said their brother, slipping through the opening and ramming the doors shut. He sniffed the air noisily.

Chloe sighed loudly. "Guess who's here?" she said to Dorothy.

Dorothy was too busy leaning over the neighbor's fence to reply. "Toto!" she called.

Chloe joined her. "Why Mrs. Ehrenkrantz would call such a huge dog Toto is a mystery to me," she said.

Harry crashed against Chloe. "Irish settlers remind me of horses," he said. "She's not anything like that little mutt in *The Wizard of Oz*."

Dorothy said haughtily, "Mrs. Ehrenkrantz loved the movie, like me. I think it was very smart of her to name her dog Toto. Besides, it's an Irish *setter* and here comes Mrs. Ehrenkrantz, so keep quiet."

Toto was prancing coltishly as she saw her owner approach. She lunged and planted two big paws on Mrs. Ehrenkrantz's shoulders, licking her face furiously.

"Kissed by a dog!" said Harry loudly, and Mrs. Ehrenkrantz laughed.

"Ain't love grand?" said Mrs. Ehrenkrantz, wiping her mouth with her sleeve. "I'm so glad to see you children. Do you think your mom would let me hire you to dog-sit?"

"For money?" said Dorothy, blushing when Chloe shushed her.

"Ten dollars for two days. I'm going away to a convention." Mrs. Ehrenkrantz bent to pet Toto, who by this time was lolling on the ground with her feet in the air.

"I'll do it!" said Dorothy, thinking that she could buy the latest twin book to add to her collection.

"I think I'm better baby-sitting for goldfish than dogs," said Chloe, who was a little afraid of Toto.

"I'll help Dorothy," said Harry, running to the back door calling, "Maaaaa! Can we baby-sit for Toto?"

Mrs. Kane emerged carrying Arney on her hip. "Do we have to keep her at our house?" she asked.

Mrs. Ehrenkrantz leaned over the fence. "Not if you don't want to," she said. "If someone could walk her in the morning and in the evening, and give her her food twice a day, she can just stay at home. I'd like to pay the children," she added.

Dorothy clasped her hands together. "Please, Mama?" she said.

"Let me talk to your father about it," said Mrs. Kane. "Eva, if I send Henry and the children over this evening, can you show them what to do?"

"Of course," said Mrs. Ehrenkrantz.

"I'll do the pooper scooper," said Harry.

"I will," said Dorothy.

Mrs. Kane laughed. "They have a fit when I change Arney's diaper in front of them, but they're fighting over a pooper scooper!"

"I'll give them lessons after dinner," said Mrs. Ehrenkrantz. "And I don't use a pooper scooper. I use newspaper."

After supper Dorothy and Harry and Mr. Kane went next door for instructions.

"I'm just not comfortable with Dorothy un-locking and locking the door by herself," Mr. Kane explained to Mrs. Ehrenkrantz. "So I'll be her little helper."

"And I'll be her big helper," piped up Harry.

"I really don't need any help," said Dorothy, "but you can keep me company if you like."

Toto followed them through the hallway into the

kitchen. She gazed longingly at her bowl as Dorothy shook some dry dog food into the dish. She set it down and watched Toto gobble up her food.

"Give her fresh water and some food, and that's all there is to it," said Mrs. Ehrenkrantz. Then she showed Mr. Kane and Dorothy how to slip the chain over Toto's neck.

"Won't she choke?" said Dorothy anxiously.

"She's used this chain since she was a baby," said Mrs. Ehrenkrantz.

Harry's eyes widened. "Was she ever a baby?" he said as they went out the front door and down the walkway.

Mrs. Ehrenkrantz handed the leather part of the leash to Dorothy. "Don't loop it over your wrist. We don't want your hand to get hurt."

Dorothy held tightly.

"Toto is going to take you for a walk," Mrs. Ehrenkrantz said.

And Toto did. She leaped joyously along the sidewalk, and Dorothy and Harry leaped after her.

"She's fast!" Dorothy called behind her. She

heard her father and Mrs. Ehrenkrantz laughing as they followed, but she didn't dare turn around.

"I told you she was like a horse," said Harry, running alongside his sister. "She's galloping!"

They passed the sign that said WALNUT SCHOOL and ran a few blocks farther. The dog took a sharp turn right and Dorothy felt the concrete under her feet change to dirt as they entered Nomahegan Park.

"She loves walking in the woods," warned Mrs. Ehrenkrantz just as Toto dove into the bushes, sniffing and circling around a patch of grass.

"Is she going to do her business there?" whispered Harry.

"Maybe not," said Mrs. Ehrenkrantz, ready to slip a wad of paper under the dog.

Sure enough, Toto rejected the spot, lunged into a patch of shiny leaves, made an about-face, and started pulling Dorothy along the dirt pathway again. Then, with a sudden shifting of her body to the left, Toto pulled Dorothy to the other side of the path, alongside a small pond.

"Are you all right, honey?" her father called. "Don't let her pull you into the water!"

"I'm fine," Dorothy said breathlessly. "I just wish she would make up her mind." Abruptly Toto squatted on the dirt path beside the pond. Mrs. Ehrenkrantz darted forward and put the wad of newspaper under Toto.

"We have to keep the park clean!" she said as they watched Toto do her business.

"Gross," said Harry. "You can have all the money, Dorothy."

Dorothy turned pale, but it didn't feel right to ask her father to do the dirty work in front of Mrs. Ehrenkrantz.

Mr. Kane read his daughter's mind. "In the beginning," he said, "would you like me to help out with the newspaper part, Dorothy?"

"Sure," said Dorothy, breathing a sigh of relief.

"Use the funny papers," advised Harry. "I like to read the comics. Toto might like it, too."

Mrs. Ehrenkrantz laughed. "Toto is not particular about which part of the newpaper you use, Harry!"

Early the next morning, Dorothy and Mr. Kane gave Toto water and fed Toto her dog food, and Toto took them on a brisk spring walk. Mr. Kane reluctantly allowed Dorothy to hold the leash, but he stayed close by. They were both panting by the time Toto dragged them to her favorite area in the woods by the pond. Toto sniffed out a spot quite quickly, and Mr. Kane did the scooping while Dorothy held her nose. Now that Mrs. Ehrenkrantz was gone, she didn't think it would hurt anyone's feelings, and Toto didn't seem to mind. Mr. Kane found a nearby trash can, and they started back home.

"See you later, partner," said Mr. Kane, shaking hands with Dorothy at the Ehrenkrantz doorway after they'd locked Toto inside.

"Bye, partner," said Dorothy as Chloe and Harry joined her for the walk to school.

"Everything come out okay?" said Chloe, laughing as she handed Dorothy her knapsack.

"Perfectly," said Dorothy, raising an eyebrow. "The ten dollars will come in handy, too."

"Papa should get half of it," said Harry.

"If you can tell me how much half of it is, I'll give it to him," Dorothy said crossly.

Harry ran his hand along a neighbor's bush. "Half of ten," said Harry uncertainly. "Is it four?"

Chloe snickered. "I guess you get it all," she said to Dorothy.

After dinner the next evening, on their last day of dog-sitting, Mr. Kane and Dorothy began their doggy duties. Chloe complained that Dorothy was getting away with murder because they were leaving right after dinner without clearing the table.

"We'll be back in time to eat dessert with you," said Mr. Kane, taking Dorothy's hand.

"I'll clear the dessert dishes," Dorothy sang out.

Toto ate her dinner like a good doggy and the three of them started walking, then running, then loping toward Toto's favorite part of the woods. Toto did her business on the business section of Mr. Kane's newspaper.

"We have her trained just right," Dorothy said happily as they headed for home.

"Like clockwork," said Mr. Kane, smiling.

Toto stopped so suddenly that Dorothy nearly toppled right over her. The dog's ears twitched. There was a rustling of leaves in the copse of trees by the pond. Toto stood perfectly still and pointed her nose in the direction of the sound.

"Hold tight," whispered Mr. Kane. "She's a hunting dog, and she smells something."

Dorothy held tight, but not quite tight enough. Toto lunged forward and tore into the underbrush, yanking the leash right out of Dorothy's hand. There was the sound of thrashing and then silence.

Dorothy looked at her father. "What are we going to do?" she whispered.

"Run after her!" said Mr. Kane, tearing into the bushes himself.

Dorothy and Mr. Kane reached the bank of the pond in record time, but Toto was already frolicking in the water.

"What is she after?" said Mr. Kane, craning his neck. "It's getting so dark out, I can barely see."

"I can," said Dorothy, squinting her eyes. "She's got a duck in her mouth!"

"Oh, good heavens," said Mr. Kane. "Toto!" he shouted. "Come here this instant!"

His tone of voice reminded Dorothy of her father's very sternest warning when Harry refused to go to bed—"Harry! Get in your bed this instant!"—only Harry usually scrambled to his feet and flopped across the bed before his father made an angry entrance. Toto didn't scramble. She waded through the pond, water up to her neck, the duck in her jaws.

"Is she eating the duck?" said Dorothy in a small voice.

"She's retrieving it," said Mr. Kane, cupping his hands around his mouth as he called the dog once more.

Toto stood still in the water, her head cocked in the air, the duck limp and motionless in her mouth. "Stay here," Mr. Kane said to Dorothy, groaning as he put one foot in the water and then the other. Water rose to the top of his thighs as he sloshed through the murky pond. "Heel," he said to Toto as he reached her. He gripped the dog's jaws and forced them open. The terrified duck flopped into the water and took off. Then Mr. Kane hooked his fingers around the dog's collar, holding on for dear life as he dragged the struggling Toto toward the bank of the pond.

Dorothy watched her father move one sodden foot after another. Suddenly a flapping of wings behind Toto propelled the hunting dog into her final lunge. Mr. Kane lunged with her and fell sideways into the water.

"Are you all right?" Dorothy shouted as she searched the surface of the water anxiously. There was a thrashing sound, a low growl, and more splashing. Dorothy squinted into the darkness. She made out the dim outline of her father's outstretched left hand, Toto's ears flapping into view, Mr. Kane's shoulders as he rose up out of the water, then his waist, his blue jeans, and finally his right hand, still hooked around Toto's collar. Her father's eyeglasses had slipped down to the tip of his nose, but he had never let go of the dog.

"I'm okay!" Mr. Kane shouted, wading slowly

through the pond until he took Dorothy's out-stretched hand and hoisted himself out of the murky water, dragging Toto with him.

Dorothy found the leather end of the leash and handed it to her father.

"Thank you, honey," said Mr. Kane, shielding himself with his hands from a shower of water as Toto attempted to shake herself dry. He started to laugh uproariously.

"What?" said Dorothy wonderingly, but she could not help laughing along with him.

"I can't believe I'm trying not to get wet!" Mr. Kane said between bursts of laughter. He took hold of the leather thong and held tightly to the chain. "Let's go, sweetie," he said, and the three of them went walking, out of the woods, onto the concrete sidewalk, past Walnut School, laughing all the way down the street.

After they had toweled off Toto and locked the Ehrenkrantz door securely, Dorothy and her father went home. He left his soaking-wet sneakers at the doorway.

"What happened to you?" exclaimed Mrs. Kane.

"Don't ask," said Mr. Kane, peeling off his jacket. "You tell, Dorothy."

"Toto took us for our usual walk," explained Dorothy, "and then she heard some ducks in the pond, and she took Papa for a swim. Papa rescued a duck that Toto was retrieving. You should have seen him!"

Mr. Kane shook his head and went upstairs. He came back into the kitchen wearing the bathrobe that Dorothy, Harry, and Chloe had helped their mother buy for his last birthday. Dorothy set a steaming mug of hot coffee carefully in front of her father. Then they all sat down to bowls of ice cream.

Mr. Kane sipped his coffee. "I took a nighttime swim and I rescued a duck," he said to the family. "It was certainly an adventure." His blue eyes found Dorothy. "I'm going to miss my walks with you, honey."

"Maybe we can take a walk some day without Toto," said Dorothy, smiling at her father. She got up out of her chair and stood behind Mr. Kane, putting her arms around him. Then she found the little bald spot on top of his head and rubbed it.

"It's for luck," Dorothy explained to Harry and Chloe. "Papa used to rub the top of Grandpa Jake's head when he was a boy."

Harry and Chloe joined Dorothy behind their father, and Mrs. Kane took Arney's small hand, and they all rubbed and they patted and they buffed the bald spot on the top of Mr. Kane's head for an abundance of good luck.

3

The Lady with the Lamp

EVERYBODY AT WALNUT School knew that Dorothy's best friend was a little girl with a big wide smile and brown curly hair named Jessica Brothers. They had met on Dorothy's very first day at Walnut School.

Dorothy had been the new girl, certain that the entire class was laughing at her because by mistake she had put poor Harry into the wrong grade. Jessica had had problems of her own! Somehow she'd managed to get her head stuck between the rungs of a wooden chair. Dorothy had held Jessica's hair ribbon while the custodian, Mr. Simpkins, sawed through the rungs of the chair. They had shared bologna sandwiches with mayonnaise at lunchtime, and they had been best friends ever since.

Their teacher, Mrs. Humphrey, certainly knew that Jessica and Dorothy were best friends. She had once joked that Jessica's last name should have been Sisters, and that Dorothy should have had the same last name. Which was exactly why Dorothy and Jessica rolled their eyes at each other when Mrs. Humphrey read the list of partners for their biography project. Dorothy was paired with Andrea Marino, not Jessica Brothers.

Andrea Marino had long blond hair and a small pouty mouth that when she smiled revealed a row of tiny white teeth. She talked a lot. To Dorothy, however, her chatter was not half as interesting as Jessica's. And her smile was not half as nice. Dorothy knew full well that she would have to spend at least one afternoon looking at Andrea's tiny teeth and listening to Andrea's stories if they were going to get the project done. Dorothy was not happy.

Mrs. Humphrey didn't seem to care. She announced, "As partners, you are to write a report about a famous female in history. Then you are to present it out loud, in front of the class."

Benny Spignolli was waving his hand. "Can I do my report on Miss Piggy?" he said.

"I think you know the answer to that, Benny. Some of you might wish to write and present a play about your heroine. For instance, if you've chosen Amelia Earhart, you might do some research and have her speak about her life as she's flying. Or have one partner be the reporter and interview the other partner. 'How does it feel to be the first woman to fly across the Atlantic, Miss Earhart?' Something like that."

Marcus Elliott, Benny's sidekick, had something to say. "Can we show her plane crashing?" said Marcus, his hands forming an airplane that dipped and crashed onto his desk.

"She was lost over the Pacific," Mrs. Humphrey

said sharply. "No one really knows what happened. Read your biography and present something interesting about your choice. Be creative!"

In the cafeteria, Dorothy handed Jessica half a bologna sandwich and took half of Jessica's peanut butter and jelly. Then Dorothy gave one of her double-dipped Oreo cookies to Jessica, who in turn gave Dorothy part of her homemade brownie. It was clear that Jessica was not happy either. They ate mournfully, as if the world had ended.

"Mrs. Humphrey did it on purpose," said Jessica, eating the bologna part of her sandwich. "She's trying to separate us. She gave me Clarice, you know. And everybody knows that Clarice has been eating chalk since she was in kindergarten."

"Does she still eat chalk?" said Dorothy, chewing on an Oreo cookie and wondering what chalk tasted like. "I know," said Dorothy. "Maybe a woman invented chalk, and the two of you can write a play about her!"

"Very funny," said Jessica. "I know she's going to want to do it on someone like the queen of England," she said glumly.

"What's so bad about that?" said Dorothy. "You could wear a crown!"

Jessica refused to feel better. "Have you seen what the queen of England looks like?" she said, shaking her head. "She's older than my grandmother. And she isn't pretty at all."

"Well, what about Andrea?" said Dorothy. "All she talks about is her stepmother, Gina, who lets her wear lipstick on the weekend and takes her places. We're going to have to do our project on Gina!"

Jessica sighed and offered Dorothy a bite of her apple. "I know!" said Jessica. "We could do our project on Eve! You know, Adam and Eve in the Garden of Eden?"

It was Dorothy's turn to shake her head. "I don't think there will be a biography on her," she told her best friend.

After school that day, Dorothy asked her mother about meeting Andrea at the library.

"I'm sure your father will drive you," said Mrs. Kane, tears filling her eyes as she chopped an onion.

"Mrs. Humphrey told us that if you put a piece

45

of white bread in your mouth while you cut an onion, you won't cry."

"Would it work the same with whole-wheat bread?" said Mrs. Kane, wiping at a tear with the back of her hand.

"Probably," said Dorothy. "Should I get you a piece?"

Mrs. Kane waved her hand in the air. "Forget about it," she said. "I'd feel like a fool with a piece of bread hanging out of my mouth. Besides, I could use a good cry."

"So could I," said Dorothy. "I have to do my project with Andrea Marino."

"Do I know Andrea?" said Mrs. Kane.

"We said hello to her and her mother at the supermarket the other day," said Dorothy. "Remember? Mrs. Marino told you that Andrea liked Breezy detergent because it made the clothes smell so nice."

"I remember," said Mrs. Kane. "A talkative woman, very friendly. I bought the detergent."

"Andrea's the same way," said Dorothy. "Yap yap yap. I wish I could be with Jessica."

"I know, honey," said Mrs. Kane, a tear running down her face. "Just give Andrea a chance. Practice being a good listener."

"How would you like to listen to her mother all day?" said Dorothy.

"I guess I wouldn't. But sometimes we have to do things that aren't pleasant." Mrs. Kane wiped a tear away with the corner of her sleeve. "Like chopping up this onion. It's making me cry, but it will make the food taste good."

"I hate onion," said Dorothy, handing her mother a tissue. "Andrea lives with her mother and her grandmother. Her parents are divorced. Her father got married again to a lady named Gina. Andrea loves Gina. She talks about her all the time."

"It's not easy being divorced," Mrs. Kane said as she scraped the mound of onion into a pan. "It's nice that she likes her stepmother."

"Gina is always doing stuff with her. Giving her manicures and taking her to the movies."

"She sounds like she's trying hard not to be the

evil stepmother," said Mrs. Kane, rinsing her hands under the faucet.

"Andrea's grandmother only speaks Italian. She picks up Andrea at school, and she calls Andrea *carina,* or something like that. She talks as much as the mother."

Mrs. Kane laughed. "The apple doesn't fall far from the tree," she said. "I'm sure Andrea's mother is happy for the support. Does she work outside the home?"

"I think she's a nurse, like Mei-Hua's mother," said Dorothy. Mei-Hua was Chloe's best friend, and Dorothy thought she was almost as nice as Jessica.

Mrs. Kane dried her hands and said, "Now that I'm finished crying, how about setting the table with me?"

"Okay," said Dorothy, taking a bunch of forks out of the cutlery drawer. She turned to look at her mother. "I'm glad you and Daddy aren't divorced," she said.

"So am I, honey," said her mother.

After supper Mr. Kane picked up Andrea and drove the girls to the library. Andrea started talking the minute she got into the car. When Mr. Kane switched on the radio, she just talked louder.

"Is this jazz?" she said to Mr. Kane. "I don't like jazz. Gina and I listen to country music."

"How nice," said Mr. Kane, pulling into the parking lot of the library.

"My dad hates country music," Dorothy said to Andrea as they got out of the car.

"How could anyone hate country music?" said Andrea.

Inside the library, Dorothy found the biography section. Andrea pulled a book off the shelf. "Monica Seles!" she cried. "I could hold Gina's tennis racket and you could interview me!"

"I'm not big on tennis," said Dorothy, reaching for another book. "Here's one about Annie Oakley."

"A cowgirl?" said Andrea scornfully. "I don't think so."

"Pocahontas?" said Dorothy, not bothering to take the book off the shelf.

"The movie was okay," said Andrea, "but I don't want to read about her."

"Emily Dickinson?" said Dorothy excitedly. "We could wear long dresses and I could borrow my grandma Rebecca's cameo and we could recite poetry!"

"Poetry?" said Andrea. "Give me a break!"

By the time Dorothy's father appeared at their table, his own books in hand, they were no closer to a decision.

"How about Eleanor Roosevelt?" Mr. Kane said, trying to be helpful. "She was married to my father's favorite president, Franklin Delano Roosevelt, and my mother just loved her."

"Never heard of her," said Andrea.

Dorothy was surprised to see her father roll his eyes, very much the way she had rolled hers at Harry when he had suggested that she do her report on Daisy Duck.

Andrea turned down Hillary Clinton with a snarl that reminded Dorothy a little of Toto when the duck had been removed from her mouth. She made a face at Louisa May Alcott. When Dorothy handed her a biography of Betsy Ross, she said, "What's so great about sewing a flag? Gina sews all of her own clothes," at which point Mr. Kane started reading at another table.

That's when Dorothy had an inspiration.

"Your mother is a nurse, isn't she?" said Dorothy.

"What's that have to do with anything?" said Andrea.

"Florence Nightingale!" said Dorothy. "And maybe we can borrow two of your mother's nurse's hats!"

Andrea thought for a moment. Then she said, "I can be Florence, and you can be one of the nurses I train."

"Okay," said Dorothy. "Can your mother get us the hats?"

"Caps," said Andrea. "The word is caps. Sure she can!"

The morning that Dorothy and Andrea were supposed to give their report, Dorothy was too nervous to eat her entire waffle. She practiced reading her script over a glass of milk and put it carefully in her knapsack so that it wouldn't wrinkle. She telephoned Andrea to remind her to bring her mother's nurse's caps. She found the flashlight that looked like a lantern at the bottom of Harry's toy chest and tested it to make sure that the batteries were working. A flip of the switch, and the lantern glowed.

"I have three paths to choose from," Dorothy said out loud. "I can be a literary woman. I can be a married woman. Or I can be a nurse." Dorothy lifted her lamp in the air.

"Or you could be nuts," said Harry, munching on cold cereal.

"I am the lady with the lamp," Dorothy said proudly.

"You are the lady with the rocks in your brain," said Harry, accidentally spitting cereal at her.

"You are probably the reason she became a nurse," said Dorothy. "Who would want to stay at home with an annoying brother like you?"

"Florence, Harry, get ready for school," said Mrs. Kane, slipping a sweater on baby Arney. "Arney and I are going to walk with you."

Dorothy sat through Marcus Elliott's report on Annie Oakley. Benny and Marcus wore cowboy hats, but Mrs. Humphrey made Marcus put away his toy rifle. "Props are fine," warned the teacher, "but I don't like weapons in the classroom."

Joshua and Marianne did their report on Queen Elizabeth I. Joshua made believe he was her father, King Henry VIII.

"Elizabeth's mother was Anne Boleyn. She was my second wife, and what a pain. I beheaded her!" Joshua raised his hand in the air and chopped down on Marianne's neck.

"You didn't chop my head off," Marianne hissed. "You chopped off my mother's. What a father!"

"I think I was a good father," said Joshua, the king. "I just wasn't a very nice husband." Joshua began to talk in detail about the rest of his wives, until Marianne interrupted him.

"It's supposed to be about me!" she said impatiently. "I was the queen of England for a long time," Marianne continued. "From 1558 to 1603, I ruled England. That's forty-five years. Back in those days, lots of people hardly lived to be forty-five years old. There were lots of diseases and babies died a lot and people didn't live to be eighty like they do today. I was seventy when I died."

"And you're still talking!" piped Benny Spignolli.

"Thank you, Joshua and Marianne. Perhaps the next time you can confer a little more with each other," Mrs. Humphrey said when they'd finished their play. "A little choppy but good," she added, winking.

Joshua started his chopping routine again until Mrs. Humphrey shushed them. "Andrea and Dorothy," she said loudly. "May we hear your report?"

Dorothy's heart started hammering as she reached under the desk for her lantern. She picked up her script and joined Andrea at the front of the room.

Andrea looked adorable. Perched on top of her

blond head was a little white nurse's cap, as cute as a button.

"Do you have one for me?" whispered Dorothy.

"I couldn't get you one," Andrea whispered back. "Anyway, you're just the narrator. *I'm* Florence Nightingale."

Dorothy didn't have time to be mad. She cleared her throat and began to read. " 'Florence Nightingale was born in Florence, Italy, in 1820. That's why her parents named her Florence.' "

Benny waved his hand furiously. "I was born in Hackensack, New Jersey! Just think," he said. "My parents could have named me Hackensack!"

Dorothy raised her voice and continued. " 'A year later, the family returned to England. When Florence was young, she wanted to take care of anything sick. Even dogs and broken dolls.' "

Andrea got down on all fours and barked like a dog. Then she made a whining noise, waved her hand feebly, and said in a weird voice, "Oh, thank you, Miss Nightingale, for fixing up my poor paw."

Dorothy felt her face flush. Impersonating a dog

definitely wasn't in the script. She raised her voice and tried to speak above the laughter. " 'Florence Nightingale liked being a nurse,' " Dorothy said loudly. " 'But her parents wouldn't let her work in a hospital. In those days, hospitals were horrible places.' "

"What a disgusting place!" cried Andrea in a phony English accent. "No daughter of mine is going to work in a gross-me-out hospital!" Andrea shook her finger at her imaginary daughter. Then, with a wave of her hand, she said to Dorothy, "You may resume speaking."

"Oh, thank you," said Dorothy, hoping that Andrea could catch the sarcasm. She cleared her voice and continued. " 'Only poor people went there, and they usually died.' "

Andrea burst out, "But I would not be stopped!" She grabbed Dorothy's lamp and held it in the air.

"You're not even a nurse yet," whispered Dorothy. "You don't need the lantern."

Andrea ignored her and lifted the lantern higher.

"Even though nurses in those days were untrained, that didn't stop me! They slept in wooden cages, you know."

"What were they, canaries?" yelled Benny Spignolli.

"Benny!" warned Mrs. Humphrey. "Please be quiet."

Andrea raised an eyebrow. "That's why my mom and dad didn't want me to be a nurse. But I didn't want to get married. Who wants to marry a crummy old boy, anyway? Not me. So I convinced my parents to let me train at a school in Germany. We got up at five in the morning."

"My dad gets up at five in the morning," said Joshua.

Andrea ignored him. "But when I got back home, my mother and sister were so mad, they hardly spoke to me. I was sad."

"My brother's mad at me," said Benny. Mrs. Humphrey gave him the eye, and he slapped his hand over his mouth.

"Boo hoo, boo hoo," sobbed Andrea, wiping

away imaginary tears. "I wish my parents wanted me to be a nurse!"

Dorothy said hastily, " 'Then Florence spent a year nursing relatives. Her father, her sister, and a dying grandmother. They all thought she was great.' "

"Except maybe for the grandmother, who died," said Andrea.

The class started laughing. Dorothy put her hands on her hips and said, "Excuse me, but that's not part of the play." She waited for the laughter to die down and said, " 'So Florence took a job at a hospital for sick gentlewomen. She didn't earn a dime. But she was good at it, and she loved her job.' "

Dorothy kept reading. " 'Then the Crimean War started, and Florence Nightingale got together a group of thirty-eight women and went to Turkey. They had turned the army barracks into an emergency hospital. And this is what Florence saw.' " Dorothy nodded at Andrea, who lifted up Dorothy's lamp again and made believe she was entering a room.

"Oh, my gosh!" said Andrea, stopping dead in her tracks. "There is no medical equipment here! Where's the furniture? Where's clean water? What a stink! What a mess! *Que puzza!*"

The class tittered, and Mrs. Humphrey stood up. She narrowed her eyes. She looked grim. "Go ahead, girls," she said.

Benny raised his hand. "What does *que puzza* mean?" he asked.

"It means 'What a stink!' in Italian. My grandmother said it just the other day when she came into my bedroom and it smelled disgusting."

"What does that have to do with Florence Nightingale?" said Benny.

"Well, we thought it was a dead mouse, but my grandmother found a moldy bologna sandwich under my bed. I don't know how it got there. And she said, *'Que puzza!'* Make believe an Italian soldier said it, Benny. There was no clean water, and there was no furniture and no medical equipment. I mean, there were no bandages! And this guy is looking down at his bloody leg covered in rags, and the sewers smelled bad, worse than my bologna sandwich. What a stink!"

The class tittered and Mrs. Humphrey stood up. She narrowed her eyes again. She looked grimmer than before. "Go ahead, girls," she said.

"It gets worse," said Andrea. "I'm walking down the hallway and . . . Hey! What's that noise?" Andrea looked bug-eyed. She jumped up on the seat of the empty desk at the front of the room. "Help!" she screamed. "A rat! A rat is crawling all over that sick man!"

Dorothy squinted at the script in her hand. Andrea hadn't read one word from their carefully prepared play.

She watched in amazement as Andrea waved her arms in mock terror. The nurse's cap trembled on her head. Dorothy felt like ripping it right off Andrea's head and throwing it out the window. Instead she read over waves of laughter, " 'This terrible place was where Florence and her nurses were supposed to work. Hundreds of wounded men arrived, starving and frostbitten. To make matters worse, some of them had bad diseases like cholera and typhus. Florence took charge. She got lots of stuff they needed, like sheets and medicines—' "

Andrea lifted up a doctor's kit. "Hellooo!" she cried, shaking the bag. "Look what I've brought with me!" Andrea took out a few empty aspirin bottles. "Here, dear, you'll feel better if you take this," she said to an imaginary soldier.

Dorothy rolled her eyes. " 'And socks and toothbrushes,' " she said stonily.

Andrea pointed to her socks and imitated brushing her teeth, at which point her cap fell over her eyes and the class started laughing again.

Dorothy gritted her teeth and continued speaking over the noise. " 'Each night she walked about four miles, visiting the soldiers and carrying her lantern.' "

Andrea swung Dorothy's lantern so hard that Dorothy had to duck. "The soldiers loved me," said Andrea. "I would speak to them or sit with them while they were dying. Some of the men kissed my shadow as I walked by."

Dorothy was glad when Benny Spignolli interrupted show-off Andrea one more time. "I wouldn't kiss your socks!" he yelled.

"Benny, another outburst like that one, and you'll be kissing the principal's office," said Mrs. Humphrey in her I-mean-business voice. "Finish up, girls."

" 'Florence continued to improve hospital conditions,' " Dorothy read. " 'She brought in better food for them to eat.' "

Andrea chomped loudly and rubbed her stomach.

" 'She set up reading and writing rooms for the men.' "

Andrea made believe she was writing a letter. "Dear Mom," she said loudly. "I was shot in the leg, but Florence Nightingale saved me. It used to stink here until she came."

" 'Queen Victoria sent her a gold and diamond brooch for a present,' " Dorothy read quickly, sighing as her partner held an imaginary mirror to her face and admired an imaginary brooch.

" 'Everybody loved the lady with the lamp,' "
said Dorothy.

"The end," said Andrea, bowing to the class.

The class started cheering, and Andrea made a
second elaborate curtsy, at which point her nurse's
cap flopped over her eyes and plopped onto the
floor by Dorothy's feet. Dorothy took one look at
the crisp white cap and couldn't resist. She
stretched one foot behind her, aimed, and kicked.
The cap skimmed across the wooden floor like a
soccer ball.

Mrs. Humphrey raised an eyebrow but looked
more puzzled than angry. "Excellent, girls," she
said, "just a little long. I think we've learned a lot
from your presentation. Dorothy, perhaps you can
retrieve the hat."

"Cap," corrected Andrea, holding out her hand
as Dorothy fetched and carried the cap over to
her.

As Dorothy sat back down at her desk, she real-
ized that Mrs. Humphrey was right. Dorothy had
learned a lot, too, about a blond girl named Andrea,

who had hogged all the props and made the play into a comedy and had tried her hardest to steal the whole show. Everybody loved the lady with the lamp indeed. Everybody except Dorothy, who vowed never to speak to Andrea again.

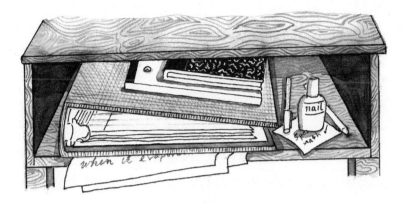

4

Dorothy's Tragedy

WHEN DOROTHY MADE a vow that she would never speak to Andrea Marino again, ever ever ever, she didn't really think that it would happen. She knew that someday she might be in a bathroom stall and need some toilet paper, and if Andrea's pink gym shoes were the ones that she spied sticking out from under the next stall, she would speak to her. Or if Mrs. Humphrey should ask Andrea to pass out the homework sheets, she would certainly take the piece of paper and say, "Thank you."

If Andrea called her on the telephone and said, "I forgot my spelling words. Could you give them to me?"—well, Dorothy knew that she could not in a million years hang up the phone in a huff, even if she wanted to. Her mother would never allow it. So when Dorothy vowed to never ever ever speak to big-shot show-off break-her-promise-to-bring-the-cap Andrea Marino again, she didn't think it would ever really happen.

That evening, as Dorothy was savoring a mouthful of chocolate-chip cookie dough ice cream, the telephone rang. Chloe was reading the ingredients off the back of the ice-cream container. Harry was grossing out everybody by sucking the ice cream off the cookie dough pieces and spitting the brown lumps back into his bowl. Mr. Kane was reading Dorothy's Florence Nightingale play as he drank his coffee.

"Harry, you're making me sick," Chloe complained as her mother picked up the telephone.

Harry didn't care. "I'm saving the best parts for last," he insisted, leaning his head over the bowl so that a piece of cookie dough might roll out of his mouth and land directly in the dish.

"Try not to look, Chloe," Mr. Kane said mildly, practicing what he preached by training his eyes onto Dorothy's paper without so much as a glance at Harry's nauseating eating habits.

"Dorothy, this is terrific," Mr. Kane commented just as his wife uttered the most terrible noise.

It was scarier sounding than the time Mama had heard over the telephone that Grandma Rebecca was in the hospital. And it was almost as scary as the scream that Harry had heard coming from the basement when his mother discovered his pet turtle Personality shriveled up in the bottom of the washer-dryer. Mr. Kane, Dorothy, Chloe, and Harry stopped everything they were doing and watched Mrs. Kane. She was crouched over as if she had an awful pain in her belly, speaking urgently into the receiver.

"When did it happen?" she said.

"What's the matter, Lillian?" Mr. Kane pushed away from the table and stood next to his wife, cupping a hand under her elbow.

Dorothy was tempted to tell her father, "Mama says not to interrupt her when she's on the telephone," but the look in Mama's eyes was chilling. And Mama was looking right at Dorothy.

Dorothy had a sudden horrible thought. What if it was Mrs. Humphrey on the telephone, reporting to Mrs. Kane that her middle daughter, Dorothy, had deliberately kicked Andrea Marino's nurse's cap across the classroom floor? Even worse, what if it were the principal? What if Mr. Torres was telling Mrs. Kane that Dorothy could not come back to school unless she had a change of attitude?

"Lillian?" Mr. Kane caught his wife's eye. She immediately held a finger in the air, saying, "Just a minute, Henry." Her mother never called her father Henry unless it was a serious situation.

"It's a tragedy," Mrs. Kane continued, drawing in a shuddery breath.

Dorothy drew in a breath of her own. She wavered. Could kicking a cap across a room be considered a tragedy?

Then her mother said, "If there's anything I can do, please let me know." She hung up the telephone and turned toward her husband. Dorothy thought she saw the glitter of a tear, heard a tiny catch in her mother's voice as she said, "We need a conference in the bathroom, Henry."

Mr. Kane followed his wife into the downstairs bathroom, which was right off the kitchen and hardly big enough for one person, much less two. Mrs. Kane shut the door firmly.

Dorothy, Harry, and Chloe hardly breathed as they listened to the muffled sounds of her mother talking, and then their father's louder exclamation, "No!"

The door opened, and Mr. and Mrs. Kane sat down at the kitchen table. Mrs. Kane started to speak. "Something awful happened today," she said quietly. "Something just tragic."

She paused, looking solemnly at Dorothy.

Eyes blazing, Dorothy blurted out, "The cap landed by my feet and I couldn't help it! So I kicked the cap, and I'm not sorry, if that was my teacher on the telephone. Only Andrea didn't bring in a cap for me and she hogged the whole show and everybody knows that I'm the one who wants to be an actress when I grow up. It just isn't fair!"

Dorothy watched in horror as a tear trickled

down her mother's face. "Sweetheart," she said, "something awful did happen to Andrea today, but it had absolutely nothing to do with you." Mrs. Kane leaned over and held one of Dorothy's hands. She took a deep breath and continued. "Andrea was hit by a car this afternoon, and she's dead."

Dorothy's eyes widened. Chloe gasped, and Harry abruptly started mixing the rest of the ice cream in his bowl. Dorothy could feel her heart beating wildly inside her chest. She could hear the loud humming of the kitchen clock, as if a giant mosquito was buzzing in her ear.

"You didn't like her, did you, Dorothy?" Harry's voice pierced the air.

"Hush, Harry," said Mr. Kane.

Dorothy looked up at the kitchen clock. The two black hands and the thin red ticking hand did a dance in front of her eyes. She blinked and tried to remember her teacher's lesson on telling time. "It's seven o'clock, isn't it?" she said in a small voice. "Andrea can't be dead, because I just saw her this afternoon. We gave our report together."

"She was walking home from school with her grandmother," her mother explained. "They stopped at the stores on Main Street to do a little shopping. That's when a car jumped the curb and hit her."

"Why did the car jump the curb?" said Harry. "Wasn't he a good driver?"

"They think he was drunk," said Mr. Kane, jerking his head toward his wife as she shushed him loudly. "Lillian, they should know. They see the advertisements on television, 'Don't drink and drive.' Well, this man had too much to drink, and he lost control of the car and ended up killing Andrea."

"What will happen to the man?" said Harry.

"Who cares about the man, Harry?" said Chloe. "Andrea's the one that died."

"I only wanted to know," he said.

"It's okay, Harry. The man will go to trial, probably," said Mrs. Kane.

"What happens to Andrea?" said Chloe, stroking her sister's back as if she were petting Toto.

"They'll have a funeral for her. And tomorrow

at school they're going to have some counselors come in to see the children. You can speak to one of them, Dorothy. They're trained to help with this sort of thing." Mrs. Kane's eyes filled with tears. "Oh, Henry," she said. "Her poor mother."

"The grandmother must be a wreck," said Mr. Kane, shaking his head.

"I don't want to speak to anybody at school," said Dorothy, jumping to her feet. "I just saw Andrea," she said, counting back the hours on her fingers. "Only five hours ago, we were up in front of the class. So she can't be dead."

Dorothy ran to her mother's bedroom. She picked up the telephone and dialed Jessica's number. It was a relief to hear her friend's cheerful voice as she sang out, "Hello! Who is this?"

"It's me," whispered Dorothy, her voice hoarse and low.

"Dorothy?" said Jessica. "You sound funny. What's the matter?"

"Andrea's dead," said Dorothy.

"What do you mean, she's dead?" said Jessica, her voice as hushed as Dorothy's.

"She was killed in a car accident," said Dorothy. There. She had told her best friend, Jessica, so it had to be real. But Jessica didn't sound as though she believed it any more than Dorothy did.

They talked some more, and Dorothy hung up the phone. She went into her bedroom. The twins in her Heavenly Hill poster smiled cheerfully at her. Dorothy wished more than ever that she could inhabit their world of proms and practical jokes and crushes on boys. She put on her favorite blue nightgown, walked into the bathroom and stuffed her dirty school clothes into the hamper, opened up the medicine cabinet and took out the bubble-gum–flavored toothpaste. Squeezing a strip of it onto her toothbrush, she brushed her teeth vigorously.

Her face in the mirror looked the same as it had that morning, round like her mother's but without the wrinkles. Her hair was still long and brown and wavy, just the way Jessica wanted hers to be. Her nose was the same straight nose that Chloe had compared to a movie star's. She was the very same person she had been at breakfast, too nervous to finish her waffle. Then she and Andrea had given their performance and Andrea had hogged the show and Dorothy had kicked the cap and the walls had come tumbling down. Everything had changed, and she couldn't yell at Andrea anymore or ignore her or complain about her to Jessica, because Andrea was dead.

Dorothy spit into the sink and rinsed out her mouth. She got into bed and pulled the blankets over her head. It was warm and dark under the covers. She could hear Harry playing with his action figures in the living room, but in her head she saw Andrea, her blond hair in a ponytail, her pouty lips parting as she talked forever.

Dorothy felt a whirling in the pit of her stomach, inching its way up her chest and into her windpipe, like the cyclone in *The Wizard of Oz* that had picked up Dorothy Gale's house and landed it on the witch, only Dorothy Kane's cyclone landed in her throat.

"Mama!" she cried, and she heard her mother run up the steps and into her bedroom.

Mrs. Kane pulled the covers down and put her arms around Dorothy. "Oh, honey," said her mother.

Dorothy started to cry. "I don't want Andrea to be dead," she sobbed, tears running down her face.

"I know," Mrs. Kane said softly, rocking Dorothy back and forth as if she were Arney.

"She can't brush her teeth anymore," said Dorothy in between sobs. "She can't put on her pajamas or say good night to her mother or talk."

"I know, honey," repeated Mrs. Kane. "It's a terrible thing."

Dorothy snuggled against her mother, her sobs gradually turning to hiccups, her tears forming a wet patch on her mother's shirt. She could hear Arney crying down the hallway.

"Your father is trying to get Arney to go to sleep," whispered Mama.

They listened as the baby's cries got fainter. They heard Harry and Chloe clump up the stairs into the bathroom. With his mouth full of toothpaste, Harry asked Chloe to read him a story.

"Dorothy reads a little better," said Harry. "But you read good, too."

Mama squeezed Dorothy's hand as her sister protested, but in a minute they heard Chloe reading.

"I don't want to die, Mama," Dorothy whispered to her mother. "I'd miss everything."

Mrs. Kane hugged Dorothy hard. "You're not going to die for a long, long, long, long time," she said, resting her cheek against Dorothy's for several minutes before she finally left the room.

Dorothy listened intently as Chloe read Harry a third story and then a fourth. She couldn't hear the words, but Chloe's steady murmur and snatches of Harry's laughter, with an occasional peep from Arney, lulled her to sleep at last.

When Dorothy walked into her classroom the next day, she found three strange people with serious expressions on their faces talking to her teacher. Mrs. Humphrey stood up in front of the class and made a speech about Andrea. Dorothy listened to the cries and noises that some of the children made, followed by a hushed silence.

Mrs. Humphrey then introduced them to a woman wearing a bright pink scarf around her neck, who was called a psychologist. The children also met a man who was as bald as Dorothy's grandpa Leon, called a guidance counselor. The social worker was a woman with deep smile lines etched around her mouth, even deeper than Dorothy's mother's lines.

Dorothy concentrated on the smudges and scratches that covered her desk. She wished with all her heart that she was home in bed, her baby blanket with the bunnies on it tucked firmly around her.

"Bad things happen to good people," said the lady with the pink scarf. "Bad things can even happen to children."

Dorothy looked at the lady. She was smiling. She looked sad and nice. But the pink scarf bothered Dorothy. It was too bright and happy for a day like today. Dorothy felt like pulling the scarf off the lady's neck.

The lady continued. "We're here to help you talk about how you feel, and we're here to talk about Andrea."

And that's what they did. Practically the whole

day, they talked about Andrea, and they talked about different people in their lives who had died. Joshua stood up and told the story about his baby brother turning blue, and how they'd rushed him to the hospital.

"But my brother didn't die, like Andrea did," said Joshua. "This morning he threw my tow truck into the toilet, and I didn't even yell at him." Joshua sat down.

Shelby stood up and said that her grandmother had died over the Christmas vacation and that Grandpa Max had cried like a baby. "Andrea let me borrow her markers," she whispered. "I left the cap off the red one, and the marker dried up." Shelby squeezed her eyes tightly shut and started sobbing.

Mrs. Humphrey put her arms around Shelby, and so did Jessica, who sat right next to her. Jessica started crying, too.

"It's okay to cry," said the guidance counselor. "And I know that it can be scary for children to see adults cry, like when Shelby saw her grandpa cry. But when we grieve, it's good to let out our feelings."

Marcus raised his hand. "I'll bet Mrs. Marino is going to cry a lot," he said.

"And her grandmother," said Kelly.

Benny raised his hand quietly. He didn't wave it wildly in the air as he usually did, or even jiggle in his seat or make funny noises to get the teacher's attention.

"Yes, Benny?" said Mrs. Humphrey, her arms around Jessica and Shelby.

"When my father died," he said slowly, "at first I didn't cry. He was sick for a long time, but I kind of got used to that. We liked to lean back on his pillow and drink ginger ale together while we watched TV."

Beth was waving her hand frantically, but Mrs. Humphrey said, "One moment, Beth. Go on, Benny."

"After he died, my mother wanted to throw out his pillow," said Benny. "But I wouldn't let her. So my mother let me keep it on my bed. That's when I cried. When I lay down with the pillow, and my father wasn't next to me anymore." Benny swallowed and made a gulping sound.

Dorothy spoke without raising her hand. "Didn't you tell me that your dad taught you how to box, Benny? Remember?"

Benny smiled. "He did. He told me I had a great right hook. But do you want to know something funny?" he said.

"What, Benny?" said Mrs. Humphrey gently.

"I never could drink ginger ale after that."

Beth was waving her hand again. "My cat died," she said. "Her name was Sherman, and she was throwing up all over the place and she was nineteen years old and my parents took her to the vet and she never came home." Beth sat down so quickly that she made a flapping noise on her seat.

"That's not as sad as a person," said Marcus.

"It's a loss," said the lady with the pink scarf. "That's what we're talking about today."

After lunch Mrs. Humphrey said, "We'll spend

the last period writing letters of condolence to Andrea's mother. A condolence is an expression of sympathy to someone who is grieving. I will send them to Mrs. Marino." She asked Dorothy to help her hand out sheets of paper.

Dorothy winced as she passed Andrea's empty desk, still brimming with notebooks and textbooks and pencils and old worksheets with A's and B's on them. The grades didn't matter anymore, nor did the tiny bottle of bright pink nail polish, the same color as the lady's scarf, that sat directly inside the desk. Dorothy could hear Andrea telling her that Gina had painted her nails over the weekend, and she could see Andrea spreading her fingers and holding out her hands, saying, "See? Gina drew little hearts on my pinkies." Her stomach did a flip-flop as she thought of poor Andrea, with little hearts on her pinkies.

Dorothy sat down to write her letter. Her pencil made a circular movement, poised above the paper to write, but what could she say to Mrs. Marino, who gabbed as much as Andrea and whose mother gabbed as much as she did? Finally she settled her pencil onto the first line and wrote:

Dear Mrs. Marino and Andrea's grandma,
I have known Andrea since I moved here a few
years ago. She was nice to me when I was new. She
always had a smile on her face. She had a kind heart.

Dorothy stopped. Did she have a kind heart? Not when she was choosing library books. Not when she deliberately didn't bring a nurse's cap into school for Dorothy to wear. Did it matter? Dorothy continued.

She loved country and western music. She loved
her grandmother's lasagna. I remember her telling
me that. She was proud that her mother was a
nurse. When we did our report together on
Florence Nightingale . . .

Dorothy lifted the pencil off the paper. She couldn't write, I was ready to brain her because she was the biggest pill in the world. She wrote,

she wore your nurse's cap. What a wonderful
actress she was!

Dorothy paused. Should she mention something about Gina? No. What if Mrs. Marino hated Gina? Dorothy wrote,

She made everybody laugh. We will miss her more than words can say.
    Sincerely,
    Her friend, Dorothy Kane.

That evening at supper, Dorothy ate a piece of her mother's honey-glazed chicken. She refused a dish of chocolate-chip cookie dough ice cream. Harry had some, but Dorothy noticed that he chewed up his pieces of cookie dough without spitting them into his bowl. She thought about Benny, not wanting to drink ginger ale anymore. She understood. She never wanted to hear the name Florence Nightingale mentioned again.

Dorothy went to bed early, with the lights on. Her mother kissed her good-night, and so did her father. They sat on the bed and looked at her solemnly.

"Would you like to talk some more, honey?" said Mrs. Kane, stroking Dorothy's forehead.

Dorothy shook her head and pulled the covers up to her chin. "Could I listen to the radio, please?"

Mr. Kane got his transistor radio from the bathroom, the one that he listened to when he was shaving.

"What would you like to hear, Dorothy?" he asked her.

"Anything but country music," she said.

Mr. Kane found a pop music station and set the radio on Dorothy's dresser. "Call if you need us," said Mama as they tiptoed out of the room. It reminded Dorothy of the time that she had had the worst case of poison ivy in the world, when everybody was quiet and the room was dark, only Dorothy had gotten better a week later.

Dorothy closed her eyes and listened to the radio. Sheryl Crow was singing "All I Wanna Do," and Dorothy's toes twitched in time to the music until she thought about Andrea. She saw Andrea in the cafeteria, handing out Christmas butter cookies. She saw her at the library, shaking her head at a book about Betsy Ross.

Dorothy squeezed her eyes shut and willed herself to go to sleep. She saw Andrea's blond head bobbing, her nurse's cap hanging over her nose. She screwed up her face and squeezed her eyes shut until they were tiny slits. "Sleep," she whispered out loud. "Sleep." She saw Andrea's cap go sailing across the classroom floor. She saw little pink hearts on Andrea's nail polish and the music kept playing, and by the time Sheryl Crow had finished singing, Dorothy was asleep.

The next day at school, there were no more strange visitors in the classroom. Mrs. Humphrey taught them a new math lesson. They read a chapter in the book they were studying. The children were quieter than usual, and Mrs. Humphrey didn't lose her temper once, not even when Benny threw a spitball that landed in Mrs. Humphrey's potted plant.

Dorothy copied her homework assignment from the blackboard. She tried not to look to the left, at Andrea Marino's desk. Someone had cleaned it out, and it stood empty and alone. Dorothy liked it better the way it had been the day before—messy and full of Andrea's things, as if she were away on vacation in Disney World and would be back in a week. Empty, it looked as if she would be away forever.

"Dorothy?" Mrs. Humphrey called her name. "Could I see you for a moment?"

Dorothy plodded to the front of the room. Mrs. Humphrey motioned for her to sit down on the chair next to her desk. She shuffled through a sheath of papers and pulled one out. It was Dorothy's letter to Mrs. Marino.

Dorothy's heart started to hammer. "Is something the matter?" she said.

"No, dear," said Mrs. Humphrey. "Not at all. It's just that Mrs. Marino has asked me to choose a letter to be read at the funeral. The children wrote so many beautiful letters that I just pulled one out of the hat, so to speak. And it was yours."

Dorothy felt a flush of warmth spread from her neck to her forehead. Her lower lip started to quiver. "I don't think they should read it," she said faintly. Her voice sounded funny, as if it were coming from far, far away. "I wasn't very nice to her on her last day here," she heard herself say. "Don't you remember?" Dorothy lowered her chin and pressed it to her chest.

Mrs. Humphrey leaned forward. She took two fingers and gently lifted Dorothy's chin. "I remember," she said. "I also remember that Andrea was her usual talkative self that day, and that she was—how should I put it?—a bit of a pill. Wasn't she?"

Dorothy examined her fingernails.

"Look at me, Dorothy," said Mrs. Humphrey.

Dorothy looked at Mrs. Humphrey. Her eyes were kind and warm like Mama's eyes, and brown like Mr. Ritter's cocker spaniel's eyes. She wore pale pink lipstick, not as bright as her mother's, and her face was a little thinner.

Mrs. Humphrey spoke. "Just because you didn't like her, Dorothy, doesn't mean you're glad she's dead. Isn't that true?"

For an instant, Dorothy was whirling in the cyclone, around and around, until it landed on the wicked witch with a thump. And then the rainbow glimmered as she pictured Andrea, barking like a dog and cowering on a chair and screwing up her nose at the awful smell. Mrs. Humphrey was right. Dorothy didn't like Andrea, not one little bit, but she wasn't glad that she was dead. Dorothy pictured Andrea taking a bow, the grin on her face as wide as the sky, her nurse's cap bobbing.

"Dorothy?" said Mrs. Humphrey. "I'm proud that you wrote such a good letter. I know it will mean a lot to the family."

"Thank you," said Dorothy in a small voice.

"And about kicking the cap across the room," continued Mrs. Humphrey.

"Yes?" said Dorothy fearfully.

"Have you ever thought of taking up soccer?"

Dorothy looked at her teacher's smiling face. Dorothy's mouth formed a grin of its own, not half as wide as Andrea's had been, not half as sweet as Arney's or as full of fun as Harry's. It was a smile just the same.

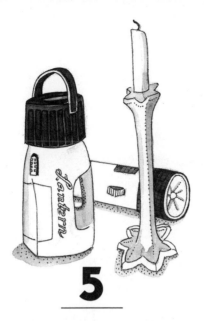

5

Dorothy's Light

On Saturday, the day of Andrea's funeral, it was raining outside.

Mr. and Mrs. Kane put on their raincoats and stood in the hallway. "You're sure you don't want to go, Dorothy?" said Mrs. Kane, clutching her umbrella.

"No, thank you," said Dorothy. "I'll stay with Aunt Sarah." Mrs. Kane's sister came up behind Dorothy and put her arms around her niece, saying, "We'll be fine here."

When Dorothy's parents had gone, Aunt Sarah put Arney in the swing and they all played board games. Then Harry lost a lot of money in Monopoly and in a fit of temper swept the pieces across the living-room floor.

"You're such a baby!" cried Dorothy, who was winning.

"We're never going to play with you again!" Chloe yelled.

Aunt Sarah ordered Harry to pick up the pieces, and Harry threw himself on the floor and started crying, which made Arney start to screech. Aunt Sarah turned red in the face and yelled, "Now you've done it, Harry. You've made Arney cry. And nobody likes a sore loser!"

Harry lay in the corner while Aunt Sarah put Arney down for a nap. Chloe started picking up the Monopoly pieces and Dorothy joined her. Harry rallied in time to put the last plastic house into the box, and by the time Aunt Sarah suggested ordering pizza for supper, he was cheerful enough to shout, "Hurray!"

Twenty minutes later, Mr. and Mrs. Kane walked

in the door. Mama handed Aunt Sarah a box of pizza. "We met the delivery man outside," she told her sister.

After they'd hung up their wet raincoats, Mr. and Mrs. Kane hugged Harry and Dorothy and Chloe as if they hadn't seen them for a long time.

"Your eyes are red," said Harry as he looked at his mother.

"So are yours," said Mrs. Kane suspiciously. "Did something happen?"

"Nothing at all," cut in Aunt Sarah, winking at Dorothy and Harry and Chloe as she divided up the pizza. "They were as good as gold."

"How was the funeral?" said Chloe.

"Very sad," said Mrs. Kane. "But we liked your letter very much, Dorothy. Andrea's father read it out loud at the service."

"I didn't write it to Andrea's father," said Dorothy, puzzled. "I wrote it to her mother." Dorothy looked worried. "Maybe I should have mentioned Gina! Andrea loved Gina, and I left her out of the letter."

"They all sat together," Mr. Kane said gently.

"The whole family. Mr. Marino and Gina and Mrs. Marino and the grandmother."

"Did you see Andrea in a coffin?" said Harry.

"Why does he always think of the worst questions?" said Chloe.

"He's curious, Chloe," said Mrs. Kane. "It was a closed coffin, Harry. But the funeral parlor was filled with beautiful flowers."

"Let's eat!" said Harry, letting his head fall back and dangling a slice of pizza above his mouth.

"You see?" said Chloe. "Now he's ready to pig out."

"He's allowed to eat," said Dorothy, patting her brother's knee. "I'll eat with you, Harry."

Aunt Sarah went home after supper, and the family gathered in the living room to watch television. Harry and Dorothy sat between their parents on the couch, and Chloe sat on the floor, holding Arney in her lap as she leaned against her father's legs. Rain pattered noisily against the picture window.

"It's cozy, isn't it?" said Harry, immediately

whooping loud enough to make Arney jump as Superman flew into the air. There was a buzzing sound and a flicker of light. The television fell silent just as the lights went off inside the house and out in the street. The Kane family sat in darkness.

"Let me get my flashlight," said Mr. Kane, pushing himself carefully off the couch so that he didn't step on Chloe and Arney.

But when Mr. Kane finally found his flashlight, he discovered that the batteries were dead. He checked the bottom drawer of the refrigerator where he kept the spare batteries, but there were none to be found.

"I know where some candles are," said Mrs. Kane, making her way across the living room floor with her arms stretched out as if she were Frankenstein's monster. "Ouch," she said crossly. "I just walked into a wall."

She made her way into the dining room and fumbled for the cabinet that held all of her best tablecloths and silverware and fancy bowls reserved for company.

"Here they are!" said Mrs. Kane triumphantly. "The candlesticks that Grandma Rebecca gave me when we got married. And they have candles in them!" She groped her way back into the living room and placed the pair of candlesticks carefully on the coffee table. Then she stepped over Chloe and Arney and settled herself onto the couch.

"Haven't you forgotten something, Mama?" said Harry. "Don't you have to light the candles?"

Mrs. Kane laughed and started the slow trek into the dining room again. Everyone listened to the sounds of drawers opening and shutting, cabinet doors slamming, and Mrs. Kane mumbling under her breath.

"I can't find any matches," she said in an exasperated voice. Arney's peeping turned to whimpering in Chloe's arms and continued even when Mrs. Kane took him and did the dipping dance in the middle of the living-room floor.

The wind started howling, and Arney's whimpers turned to wails. Harry said from the center of the couch, "This is a little scary."

Arney howled louder. Mrs. Kane bent her legs

and continued her rhythmic swooping, dipping a little deeper now, up and down, up and down. Arney continued screeching.

Mr. Kane pushed himself off the couch once again and said, "I'll go get him a bottle."

"Don't go," said Harry. "I'm all alone."

"I'm here," said Dorothy, leaning close to her brother.

Chloe got up off the floor and sat on the other side of Harry. "I'm here, too," said Chloe.

"I'll be back in a second," said Mr. Kane.

"If the power stays off, all my food will spoil," fretted Mrs. Kane.

"It will be back on soon," Mr. Kane called over his shoulder. He returned with a bottle and handed it to his wife. "I hope he'll drink it ice cold," he said, "because I can't heat it up."

Mrs. Kane wedged herself next to Chloe and gave Arney the bottle, murmuring, "There, there," as the baby shuddered and sucked.

"There, there," said Harry, leaning against Dorothy.

"There, there," said Dorothy, leaning against

Harry. Suddenly she sat forward and shouted, "I think I can help!" Dorothy found her way in the blackness, creeping slowly up the stairs into her bedroom.

"Be careful, honey," called Mr. Kane as she fumbled in the darkness for her knapsack.

"I will!" called Dorothy, pulling the lantern out of the knapsack, untouched since the day she and Andrea had given their play. Dorothy switched on the lamp and walked downstairs into the living room, sweeping the beam of light across her family. Arney turned his head ever so slightly, blue eyes wide and unblinking as he removed one of the hands that clutched the bottle and waved at the beam of light.

"My hero!" said Mrs. Kane as Dorothy set the lantern next to the candlesticks on the coffee table and sat down between her brother and sister.

"The lady with the lamp," said Harry.

"Florence Nightingale," said Chloe, "saving the day!"

"Poor Andrea," said Dorothy, her eyes welling up with tears.

Harry put his arms around Dorothy, and Chloe knelt on the floor in front of her sister, joining Harry in a circle of hands. Arney continued to wave one fist at the light as the whole family gathered around Dorothy in a flurry of hugs.

"Do you know who we haven't seen in a while?" said Mama at last.

"Jessica!" said Harry.

"You're right!" said Dorothy, her face lighting up.

"Why don't you invite her over to play tomorrow?" said Mrs. Kane.

They sat in the living room for a long, long time. Harry told five knock-knock jokes in a row, and Chloe imitated Arney gurgling, and Mr. Kane told a story about when he was a little boy. And when the television and the streetlights and the house lights went on again, Dorothy ran to the telephone to call her best friend, Jessica.

6

Toto Rides Again

ONE WARM SUMMER morning, a few days after school had ended, Dorothy, Harry, and Chloe were playing in the backyard. Mrs. Ehrenkrantz waved to them over the fence and shouted, "Yoo hoo! Yoo hoo!"

"She wants something," Chloe predicted under her breath.

"I love Yoo Hoo!" said Harry, jumping up and down in anticipation of his favorite chocolate drink.

Chloe snorted. " 'Yoo hoo' means hello, Harry,"

she said in the snippy tone of voice that so often made Harry take the last chocolate-chip cookie and eat it noisily in front of her face.

Dorothy put down the pad of paper she had been using to record the number of flowers that grew in their garden. Harry had learned how to "estimate" at school by looking at jars full of jelly beans, paper clips, nails, pretzel sticks, and marbles and then guessing the number of objects in the jar. Harry, Dorothy, and Chloe were estimating the number of pink, white, and red geraniums that lined the house.

Mrs. Ehrenkrantz leaned over the fence. "Is your mother around, honey?" she said to Dorothy. "I need you to take care of Toto again for the next couple of days if that's possible. I have to go to Florida."

"Dorothy's already bought her Heavenly Hill twin books with the money you gave her," said Harry. "She doesn't need any more money."

"I do, too!" protested Dorothy. "I'll ask my mother."

"Maaaa!" Harry bellowed at the back door before Dorothy could make a move. "Dorothy wants to make more money! And bring me a Yoo Hoo, please. I thought Mrs. Ehrenkrantz had one!"

"Harry," Dorothy whispered directly into his ear, "you are the most embarrassing brother in the world."

Mrs. Kane slid open the back door and came outside, carrying Arney on her hip. "Did someone named Harry Kane holler?" she said, setting the baby on his tummy in the portable playpen.

"Hello, Lillian," said Mrs. Ehrenkrantz. "I have to make arrangements for my mother to enter a nursing home in Florida, and I was wondering if Dorothy could take care of Toto for me while I'm away. She did such a wonderful job the last time."

"Toto took my father swimming," volunteered Harry.

"Pardon?" said Mrs. Ehrenkrantz in a puzzled voice.

Chloe whispered into Harry's other ear, "They never told her, big mouth."

"Hank and Dorothy enjoyed it immensely," Mrs. Kane said hastily. "Taking care of Toto, I mean. I'm sure it will be fine."

Harry stood beside his mother, repeating the words "Yoo Hoo" as he performed a little hopping dance from foot to foot.

"I don't have any more Yoo Hoos, Harry," Mrs. Kane said crossly. Her voice softened as she turned toward her neighbor. "I'm sorry to hear about your mother, Eva."

"She's gotten so frail," said Mrs. Ehrenkrantz sadly. "She just can't live alone anymore."

"We visited a nursing home with my class last year," said Dorothy. "We gave out chocolate-chip cookies."

"Dorothy made an old man cry," piped up Harry.

"She reminded him of his wife," Mrs. Kane explained over Dorothy's protests. "He started to cry."

"The psychologist who visited our class said that it's good to cry when someone dies," said Dorothy, glaring at her brother.

"Andrea's dead," said Harry, smiling widely at Mrs. Ehrenkrantz.

"Oh!" said their neighbor, startled by Harry's broad smile.

Dorothy sighed. "It's okay to smile and laugh, too," she said. "The lady at school said different people do different things when someone dies. Harry smiles."

"I do not!" Harry said crossly. "I didn't smile when Personality died."

"Well," said Dorothy, "you smile when we talk about Andrea. And it seems weird to people who don't know you."

Harry leaned over Arney's playpen and grabbed hold of his brother's hand, swiping at a butterfly that flitted nearby. "See that butterfly, Arney? Maybe that butterfly will fly up to heaven and visit Andrea," he said.

Dorothy looked at Harry. Sometimes he was such a dumb brother that she and Chloe couldn't stand it. But sometimes out of his six-year-old mouth popped the smartest ideas. She watched the butterfly light on a geranium and flutter into Mrs. Ehrenkrantz's yard. Toto sprang into action, jumping at the flying insect, but the butterfly flew out of reach. Dorothy was glad. After all, Harry could be right.

Dorothy was happy for the chance to earn some more money. She had already read the two new Heavenly Hill twin books that she had purchased with her dog-sitting money, and now she had another book in mind.

Dorothy and her father decided that, to be on the safe side, they would walk Toto in the opposite direction of Nomahegan Park, past the Ehrenkrantz house into town. Mr. Kane did not fancy taking another bath with a dog and a duck in a pond, and Dorothy had agreed. And as they hadn't told Mrs. Ehrenkrantz about Toto's adventure, they didn't want to take any chances on a repeat performance.

The next day after supper, Mr. Kane and Dorothy fed Toto, put on her leash, and took her outside for her evening walk. Toto tried to drag Dorothy in the direction of the park, but Dorothy persevered. They headed down Walnut Street past several houses in a row and made a left turn onto Elm Street.

"Do they call this street Elm Street because this is an elm tree?" said Dorothy, fingering one of its green leaves.

Mr. Kane laughed. "Someone is playing a joke on us," he said. "These are oak trees, for sure. In the fall, these lawns will be covered with acorns."

"Maybe they thought that Elm Street sounded better than Oak Street," said Dorothy, smiling. "Or maybe there's a hero named Hubert Elm and they named the street after him."

They walked a little farther until Toto began her circling dance on a patch of ground in front of a tumbledown cottage. Its front yard was an over-grown jumble of garden. Black-eyed Susans mingled with daylilies, and a spread of white impatiens was surrounded by a stretch of sweet alyssum. There was no lawn to speak of, just a mass of weeds and feverfew and early summer wildflowers that

Toto obviously admired. The doorway of the house still sported an old Christmas wreath, and the windows were hung with Halloween decorations.

"Don't do your business here, Toto," muttered Mr. Kane as he tried to pull the straining dog away from her chosen spot in front of the cottage. "Mr. Garland will eat us alive."

"Harry calls Mr. Garland 'wild thing,' " said Dorothy, peering at the doorway. "Harry says he looks like the monster in his favorite book."

"Get that mutt off my property!" An old man appeared on the front porch, his wild white hair waving in the breeze as he shook a plastic baseball bat at them.

"Let's go, Toto," said Mr. Kane, dragging the dog a few feet until Toto gave up and continued walking. "Sorry, Mr. Garland!" he shouted.

Mr. Garland waved his bat again and disappeared inside the cottage.

Dorothy breathed a sigh of relief. "This walk is almost as exciting as the time Toto took you swimming!" she said to her father.

"Heaven forbid!" said Mr. Kane, handing the leash back to Dorothy.

By the time they reached the row of shops on Main Street, Toto was circling in earnest again. Her gutter of choice was directly outside Munz's Delicatessen.

Dorothy loved the deli. Directly inside the door, next to a rack of newspapers, was a long row of glass canisters filled to the brim with candies— licorice whips, bubble gum, jawbreakers, caramels, lollipops, all for a nickel each. Dorothy handed her father the leash and peered inside the store. Staring back at her, his nose pressed against the plate-glass window, was none other than Benny Spignolli.

Startled, Dorothy jumped away quickly, only to be greeted by the sight of Toto in her squatting position. "Not here," moaned Dorothy. "Not now!"

"Gross me out!" called Benny Spignolli from the doorway of the delicatessen, waving a sandwich in his hand. "My brother and I are going to sue you, Dorothy Kane, for ruining our supper! I'm looking out the window in the middle of biting into my turkey sandwich and what do I see? A dog making a pile of doo-doo. Who's going to clean that up?"

"My father," said Dorothy, hoping that her cheeks looked flushed from exercise instead of embarrassment. Her eyes trained on the sky, she shifted from foot to foot as her father cleaned up the mess that Toto had made.

"How's it going, Benny?" Mr. Kane said mildly, dumping Toto's package in the garbage can as he handed Dorothy the leash. "Ready to go, Dorothy?"

Dorothy raced ahead of Toto, Mr. Kane trotting behind her. "Where's the fire?" he called.

"Let's cross the street and go home," Dorothy said in a low voice as her father caught up to her.

Mr. Kane chuckled. "An animal moving its bowels is totally natural," he said to Dorothy.

"Gross me out," said Dorothy, eyes on the DON'T WALK sign. "Toto may be totally natural," she said to her father, springing forward as the sign flashed WALK. "But Benny Spignolli is definitely not!"

* * *

The following day it was so hot and sunny that Harry tried to talk his mother into giving him an egg. "I bet we could fry it on the sidewalk!" he said excitedly.

"Harry Kane," said his mother, "I am not wasting a perfectly good egg so that you can fry it on the sidewalk."

Dorothy, however, had better luck convincing her mother that Toto needed some fresh air and company. Dorothy, Harry, Chloe, and Mrs. Kane, wheeled Arney in his carriage around the block until he fell asleep, and picked up Toto on the way back.

"As long as you let us nap," said Mrs. Kane, positioning Arney in the shade of a tree and settling into a lounge chair.

"As long as you let me read," said Chloe, settling into her own chair.

Dorothy found an old tennis ball in the basement. They played fetch and catch until Toto refused to play anymore and lay down on the grass next to

Arney. Toto lolled happily as Harry and Dorothy petted her soft red coat and tickled her belly.

"She's bored with the ball," said Harry, springing up off the grass. "I'll find her a stick."

"She's hot," said Dorothy. "Look at the way she's panting."

"She's thirsty," said Harry, "and I need a snack. Let's go get her some water, and then I can find her a stick to play with."

Dorothy followed Harry into the kitchen as he opened the sliding door. Toto followed Dorothy.

"Hey!" said Dorothy. "Mama's not going to like it that Toto's inside."

Harry shrugged. "So let's give her a drink and get out of here. Mama's sleeping."

Dorothy found an old plastic bowl and filled it with water.

"You can get us a drink and a snack," said Harry, "and I'll get Toto a stick."

Dorothy started grumbling that she wasn't Harry's slave, but her stomach was rumbling, too.

She took another dish out of the cabinet, filled it with pretzels, got two juice boxes out of the refrigerator, and set them all on a tray the way her mother would have done it.

Then she noticed Toto's bowl of water, untouched on the kitchen floor.

"Toto, come and get your water," she called.

Toto didn't come.

Dorothy walked into the living room. Through the window she could see Harry foraging in the front yard for just the right stick. The front door was standing wide open.

"Harry!" Dorothy shouted from the doorway. "Where's Toto?"

Harry stood in the middle of the yard, his mouth hanging open. "Isn't she with you?" he said.

"You never closed the door!" cried Dorothy, running down the walkway. She shielded her eyes from the sun and peered to the right. She peered to the left. "Toto!" called Dorothy, her heart thumping in her chest.

"Toto!" cried Harry, the perfect stick for fetching clutched in his hand.

Mrs. Kane appeared in the doorway. "Don't tell me you've lost Toto!" she said.

Chloe arrived. "You've lost Toto?" she repeated.

"Toto!" shouted Dorothy, praying fervently that Toto would bound into sight with her ears flapping and her tongue hanging and her tail wagging. Mrs. Ehrenkrantz would never forgive her if she didn't.

"Toto!" called Harry, cupping his hands around his mouth. He turned toward Dorothy and said to her mournfully, "I guess you won't get your money this time."

"It's your fault! And I'm going to find her!" Dorothy said, marching down the street.

"I'll help," said Chloe, running alongside of her.

"I thought you were afraid of dogs," yelled Harry, standing forlornly beside his mother.

"We're more afraid of you, Harry," Dorothy yelled back as they parted bushes and peered into backyards.

"They always leave me behind," Harry said mournfully.

"Did you leave the front door open?" said his mother. She sighed. "What on earth am I going to tell Mrs. Ehrenkrantz if we can't find Toto?"

Harry hung his head. His shoulders drooped. There was shouting in the distance, and his ears pricked up as if he were Toto. "Do you think they see her?" he cried, jumping up and down. Mrs. Kane clasped her hands together in prayer.

"We've found her! We've found her!" they heard the girls calling.

"They've found her!" cried Harry. "I knew they would!"

Harry and his mother watched as Dorothy and Chloe dragged a tail-wagging Toto up the street.

"We spotted her in the bushes," panted Dorothy.

"Thank goodness," said Mrs. Kane. "Let's get her inside."

Dorothy, Harry, Chloe, Mrs. Kane, and Toto walked back into the house. Dorothy plopped down on the couch, exhausted. She wiped the back of her sleeve across her perspiring face.

Harry sat next to her, leaning his head on her shoulder. "Are you still mad at me?" he said.

"Yes," said Dorothy, but she reached out and rubbed the top of his head.

Wails from the baby monitor made Mrs. Kane jump. "Arney's up!" she cried, running out of the room.

"Hello, family!" Mr. Kane called a minute later as he walked through the front door. "The mail's all delivered and I'm home!"

Dorothy, Chloe, and Harry gathered around their father and began to tell him about Toto's escape.

"I headed for the park because I knew it was her favorite spot," said Dorothy.

"And we found her in the bushes before we even got to the school," continued Chloe.

"I helped," said Harry.

"You helped lose her!" cried Dorothy as Toto clambered up from the floor and stood with her nose to the door.

"Now she wants to go home," said Harry.

"Can you blame her?" said Mr. Kane, laughing as he walked up the stairs. "I'll change my clothes, and we'll take her back."

Dorothy sat by the doorway and stroked Toto's reddish fur. "Running away from me like that, you silly girl," she murmured. "We'll take you home in a minute."

From the ceiling above them, they heard their father as he walked across the bedroom floor. There was an excited shout and a loud thumping as he bounded out of the room and came to a halt at the top of the stairs. "Everybody come up here this instant!" Mr. Kane hollered. "And get your mother!"

Harry raced over to the sliding glass doors and opened them, shouting, "Mama, come quick!"

Dorothy and Chloe ran up the steps, Toto loping after them.

"What's the matter?" said Dorothy as she rushed into the room.

"What's up?" said Harry, stopping abruptly behind Dorothy.

"Are you hurt, Henry?" cried Mrs. Kane as she hurried into the room with Arney bobbing in her arms.

But Mr. Kane was smiling, one arm extended, one index finger pointing at a reddish-colored Irish setter that looked exactly like Toto, sleeping on the carpet beside the bed.

"Two Totos?" cried Dorothy, stooping to peer into the sleeping dog's face.

"They look exactly alike!" said Chloe, stepping back a pace.

"Twin Totos!" cried Harry, hopping from foot to foot.

But it soon became evident that the two dogs were different, with two sets of licenses hanging from their collars. The second Irish setter, whose nameplate said SHAWNEE, lived a few blocks away on High Street.

Mr. Kane picked up the telephone and called the owner. "Hello," he said, "I believe we have your dog at our house by mistake." Mr. Kane chuckled into the receiver. "I'll do that," he said. Then he hung up the telephone, said, "Come on, Shawnee!" to the dog that wasn't Toto, and led her downstairs. "Stay here until your owner comes," said Mr. Kane, and Shawnee sat down.

Everyone gathered around Toto, who had awakened to all of the noise and excitement and accepted a thousand Kane pats and strokes, rolling onto her back with her legs in the air.

"She's happy," said Harry as he rubbed Toto's tummy.

Dorothy stroked her gently until Toto's mouth turned up at the edges. "She's smiling!" cried Dorothy, looking around the bedroom at Harry's shining face and at her sister Chloe's big brown eyes, at her father, grinning widely as his glasses slid down his nose, and at Arney's sweet round cheeks as her mother held the baby's hand and they petted Toto together.

Toto shook her body from side to side and howled so loudly that Arney jumped in his mother's arms. Arney's eyes grew wide and his head bobbed gently and from his mouth came a sound that was clear and strong and bubbling.

"He's laughing!" cried Dorothy, and the whole family joined him so that laughter echoed from wall to wall, louder and louder, filling the Kane household and spilling out the windows.